Elizabeti's Doll

by STEPHANIE STUVE-BODEEN

illustrated by CHRISTY HALE

SCHOLASTIC INC.
New York Toronto London Auckland Sydney
Mexico City New Delhi Hong Kong

ISBN 0-439-07974-8

Text copyright © 1998 by Stephanie Stuve-Bodeen.
Illustrations copyright © 1998 by Christy Hale.
All rights reserved.
Published by Scholastic Inc., 555 Broadway, New York, NY 10012,
by arrangement with Lee & Low Books, Inc.
SCHOLASTIC and associated logos are trademarks and/or registered
trademarks of Scholastic Inc.

12 11 10 9 8 7 6 5 4 3 2 1   9/9 0 1 2 3 4/0

Printed in Mexico   49

First Scholastic printing, January 1999

Book design by Christy Hale
Book production by The Kids at Our House
The text is set in Octavian.
The illustrations are rendered in mixed media.

For Tim, Bee, and Tangelo.
Asante sana to Bobbi and the village of Malula—S.S.B.

For Elizabeth Humphreys, my dear Betsy, with love, friendship,
and fond memories of our doll days—C.H.

Elizabeti had a new baby brother named Obedi. Elizabeti watched Mama take care of him and she wanted to care for her own baby.

She didn't have a doll, so she went outside and picked up a stick.
She tried to hug it, but it poked her and she dropped it on the ground.

Then Elizabeti picked up a rock. It was just the right size to hold and it
didn't poke Elizabeti when she hugged it. She kissed the rock and named it Eva.

When baby Obedi had a bath, he splashed and got Mama wet.

When Eva had a bath, she behaved very nicely and only splashed a little.

Mama fed Obedi and he gave a loud "Brrrrp!"
Elizabeti fed Eva, but she was too polite to burp.

Mama changed the cloth wrapped around Obedi's bottom and it was very messy!

Elizabeti was very relieved to find that Eva's bottom was still clean.

When Mama did her chores, she tied Obedi onto her back
with a bright cloth called a kanga.

When Elizabeti did her chores, she also tied Eva onto her back with a kanga. Mama had to help a little.

Elizabeti went to visit her friend Rahaili. Rahaili laughed
when she saw that Elizabeti had a rock for a doll.

But Rahaili didn't have a doll either, so when Elizabeti left,
Rahaili found her own rock and named it Malucey.

When Elizabeti got home, it was time for her to get water from the village well. She took Eva out of the kanga and laid her on the ground near some other rocks, so she wouldn't be lonely.

Then Elizabeti wrapped the kanga into a small bundle, put it
on top of her head, and placed the water jug on top of the kanga.
This was how she always carried water and other heavy things.

Elizabeti soon returned with the water and took it to her sister Pendo inside the cooking hut where all the family's meals were made.

Then Elizabeti ran outside to get Eva. But Eva was gone!
Elizabeti looked all around, but she couldn't find Eva.

Mama found a new rock and gave it to Elizabeti. Elizabeti shook
her head when she saw it. The rock was just a rock.

Pendo also brought Elizabeti a rock, but it wasn't Eva either.

Elizabeti was very sad and sat quietly until it was time
to help Pendo in the cooking hut.

The family had rice for dinner every night, and it was Elizabeti's job to
put the pot of rice on the fire pit, which was made of three large stones.

Elizabeti sadly filled the pot with water and set it on the stones to boil. But one of the stones wasn't a stone at all. It was Eva!

Elizabeti called for Mama and together they moved the pot of water and rolled Eva away from the fire. Although Eva was a bit dirty, she hadn't been hurt.

Pendo ran outside to get a new stone for the fire pit, which is just how poor Eva had become lost.

Eva sat quietly while Elizabeti cleaned her off and hugged her.

At bedtime, Mama sang a lullaby and rocked Obedi in her arms until he fell asleep. Elizabeti sang a lullaby too, but she fell asleep before Eva did.

Mama covered Elizabeti and Eva with a blanket. She smiled and thought that, one day, Elizabeti would make a fine mother. Eva thought so too.

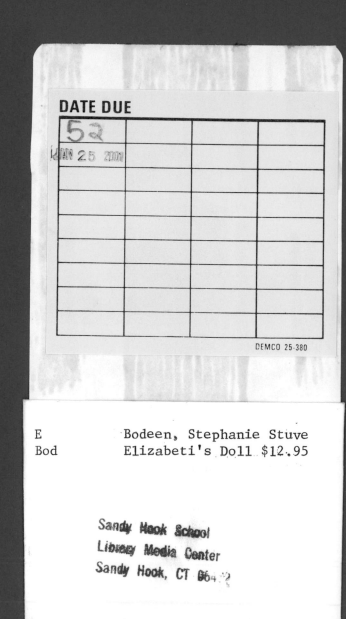